SKY, SEA, THE JETTY, AND ME

SKY,
SEA,
THE JETTY, AND ME

LEONARD EVERETT FISHER

MARSHALL CAVENDISH · NEW YORK

This book is for the loves of my life
my constant wife
Margery
our wonderful children and grandchildren
The Aldorotys: Julie, Robert, Lauren, and Michael
The Plotners: Susan, Judah, Samuel, and Jordan
The Fishers: Pamela, James, Gregory, and Danielle

Text and illustrations © 2001 by Leonard Everett Fisher. All rights reserved.
Marshall Cavendish, 99 White Plains Road, Tarrytown, NY 10591
Library of Congress Cataloging-in-Publication Data
Fisher, Leonard Everett.
Sky, sea, the jetty and me / Leonard Everett Fisher.
    p.   cm.
Summary: A young boy describes how a storm sweeps over the ocean jetty
where he likes to spend time.
ISBN 0-7614-5082-3
[1. Ocean—Fiction. 2. Jetties—Fiction. 3. Thunderstorms—Fiction.] I. Title.
PZ7F533 Sk 2001 [E]—dc21   00-057014

The illustrations are acrylic paintings.
The text is set in 18 point Galliard.
Printed in Italy
First Edition
6 5 4 3 2 1

The Sea! the Sea! the open sea!
The blue, the fresh, the ever free!
Bryan Waller Proctor (1787–1874)

Low tide and daylight were my tide and time. The jetty was my place. There I sat, in the cockpit of the rocks, watching the ships and the ever-rolling sea.

Most people who lived near the jetty were too busy to listen to the sounds of the sea, the endless beat of the breaking surf slapping the rocks or crashing into the seawall. And only gulls eyed a thousand frantic shiners trying to escape the netters.

Fog kept sensible people off the jetty. If I could not see the end of the jetty from the beach, I would stay away. The dull clank of the fog bell, echoing through the mist, was warning enough.

Now, at noon, there was little sun in the dreary sky. Summer was playing itself out. School was not far off. Usually, the clear, dry days of August held hints of the coming fall. But not now. Now it was becoming too dark for noon, yet it was the wrong season for a storm.

A breeze began to push the clammy air from one side of the bay to the other. In minutes, choppy waves hammered the seawall with foamy spray. A complaining gull challenged the wind. Its succulent dinner of silvery shiners, yet uncaught, would have to wait.

My eyes smarted from the wind-whipped brine. And through the sting I saw fingers of lightning jab a distant beach. A rusty crab darted out of a shadowy crevice, looking for a better place to hide.

The sea heaved, twisted, and smashed into the jetty. A misty squall born in the open sea and pushed by a phantom engine thundered toward me. A gust of wind pushed me against the slippery rocks. The fog bell clanked. Day became night at noon. It was time to leave the jetty—fast!

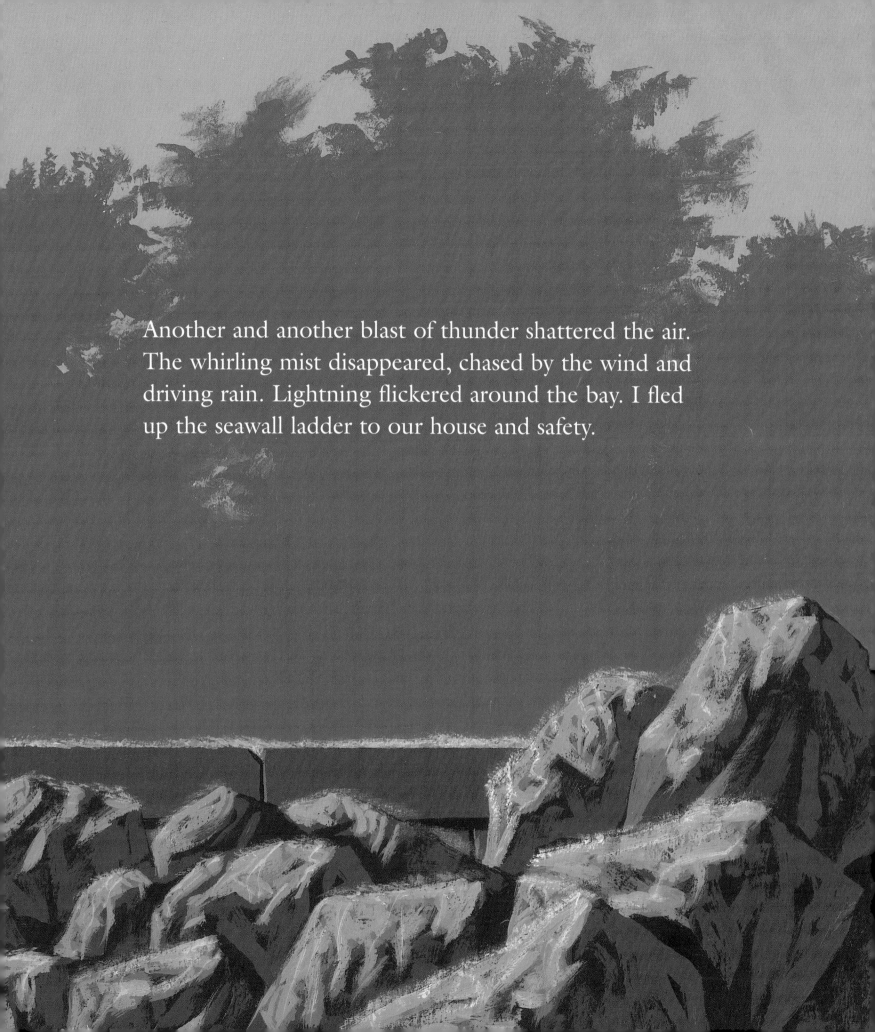

Another and another blast of thunder shattered the air. The whirling mist disappeared, chased by the wind and driving rain. Lightning flickered around the bay. I fled up the seawall ladder to our house and safety.

Soaked, dripping, and breathless, I stood behind a rain-streaked window staring at yet another crackling line of lightning. This one leaped out of the watery blackness above and slammed into the lighthouse roof next-door. The rain in its wake turned into steam.

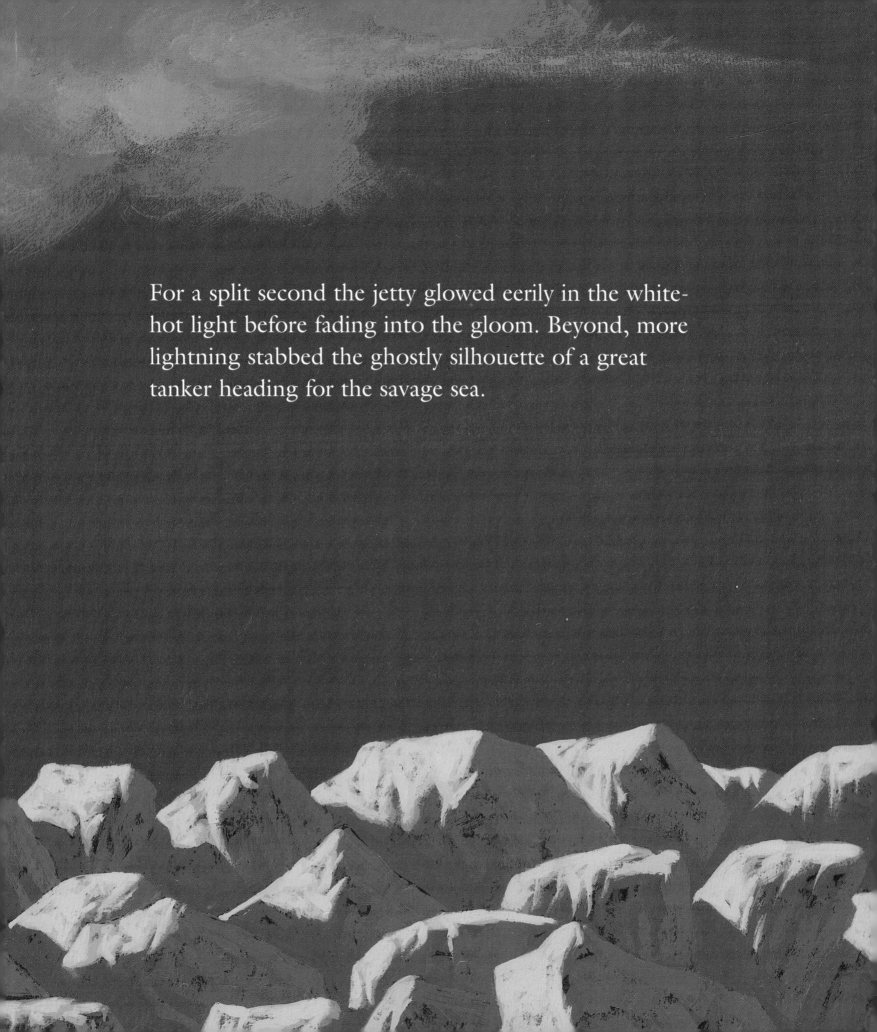

For a split second the jetty glowed eerily in the white-hot light before fading into the gloom. Beyond, more lightning stabbed the ghostly silhouette of a great tanker heading for the savage sea.

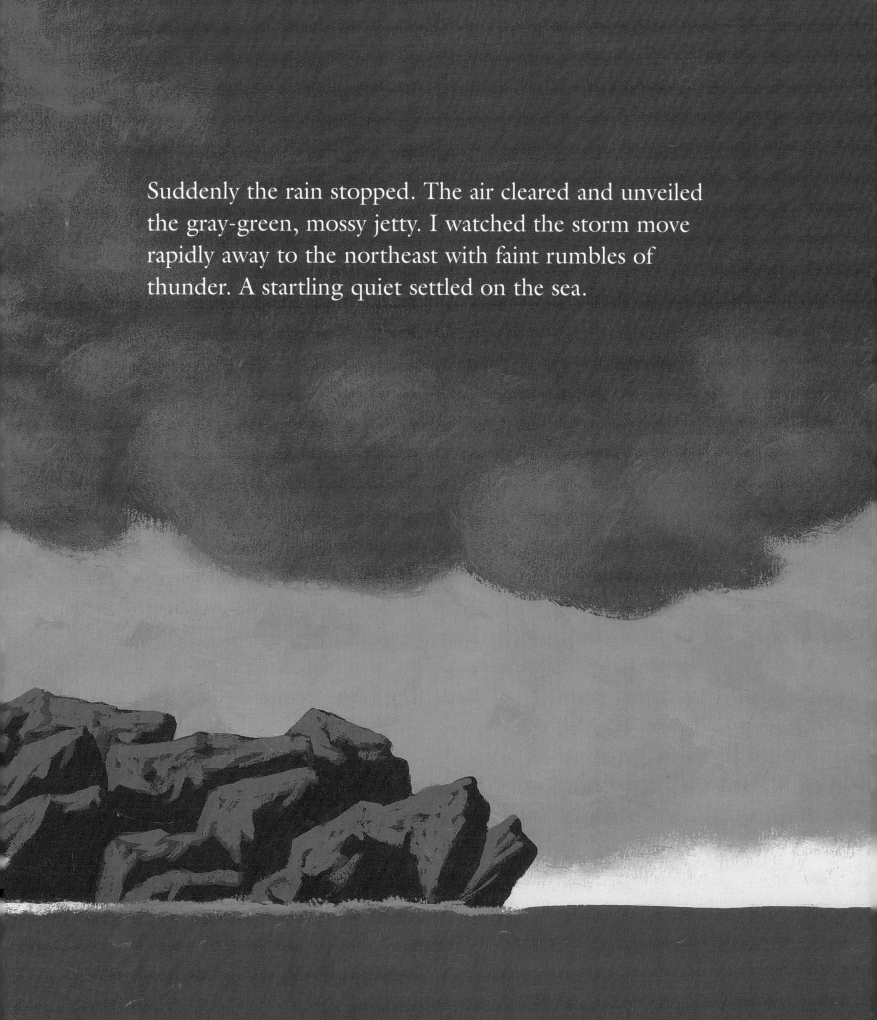

Suddenly the rain stopped. The air cleared and unveiled the gray-green, mossy jetty. I watched the storm move rapidly away to the northeast with faint rumbles of thunder. A startling quiet settled on the sea.

The sun broke through and spread its heat over the water.
Silent and spent from its wild struggle, the sea rested.

The jetty stood bathed in the brightness of the clear afternoon. Once again, I could sit in the cockpit of the rocks and watch the ships and the ever-rolling sea.

ABOUT THE AUTHOR

Leonard Everett Fisher spent his early years in Sea Gate, a Brooklyn, New York, seashore community. There, on a rocky breakwater at Norton's Point that still indicates where Lower New York and Gravesend Bays run into the Atlantic Ocean, he sat for hours, becoming a keen observer of the sea around him. Following his World War II military service and graduation from Yale University, he has illustrated some 260 children's books, authoring about 85 of them. He has, from time to time, recalled the jetty in his books for young readers and in his easel paintings. He has been the recipient of a number of honors including the University of Minnesota's Kerlan Award, the Medallion of the University of Southern Mississippi, a National Jewish Book Award, the Regina Medal of the Catholic Library Association, the Washington Post/Children's Book Guild Nonfiction Award, the Christopher Medal for Illustration , the Premio Grafico Fiera di Bologna, the Arbuthnot citation of the American Library Association, the Joseph Pulitzer Scholarship in Art, the Yale University School of Art's John Ferguson Weir Prize and William Wirt Winchester Traveling Fellowship. His art and papers are represented in numerous public and private collections throughout the United States. Leonard and his wife, Margery, a retired school librarian, have lived in Westport, Connecticut, another waterfront community, for many years.